Charlie the Chongololo

Adventures of a Giant African Millipede

The Dramatic Rescue

Pamela and Michael Collier

Illustrated by Dilys Drewett

ISBN-13: 978-1508634690
ISBN-10: 1508634696

Published by Collier Creations in both paperback and e-book formats.

Details of other books published by these authors are available on the series website:

http://colliercreations.weebly.com

For Sienna

Meet our new friend!

He lives in an exciting part of the world, and is a contented little creature who enjoys fresh air and sunshine.

Everyone likes Charlie. This is the story of a special day in his life.

One morning, Charlie wakes up early, and looks out of his front door.

It is a beautiful sunny morning. Most days are fine and sunny in Zimbabwe where he lives.

His home is No. 1 Zambezi View. From there he can look down on the great river that runs through Africa.

It is hot and wet, but chongololos love that sort of weather.

Now it is time for his morning walk, and so Charlie trots off along the path towards the river.

Having 120 legs helps him to move faster, and exercises his many muscles.

He reaches the high cliff above the river, and strolls along it, admiring the view.

But why is he holding an umbrella on such a sunny day?

This is not rain! He is right by the Victoria Falls and is being soaked by the spray from the mighty waterfall.

All around him the trees and plants look very healthy, because of the abundant water.

Along the way, he calls cheerily to those he meets.

The first is a large grey bird with a stern expression.

"Good morning, Mr Lourie," Charlie says politely.

The bird simply puts his beak in the air, and shouts "Go away! Go away!"

Further on, he spies his friend Micky, leaping from branch to branch above him.

"Hi, Charlie," he calls. "Lovely weather for a bit of gymnastics!"

Charlie waves back.

Then he notices a group of chongololos looking at the view.

There is a father, mother and little youngster, as well as several of their friends.

They have come a long way across Africa to see the famous Victoria Falls.

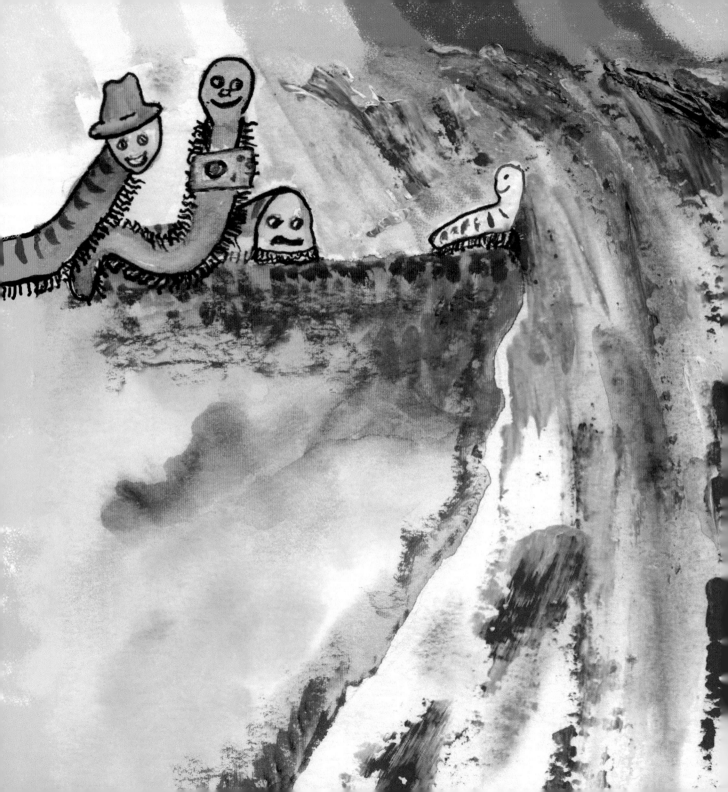

The father is trying to take a photo of the child standing on the edge of the cliff.

"Big smile, please, Chipo!"

But the spray has made the rocks very slippery.

Suddenly the small chongololo slips.

She falls over the edge of the cliff.

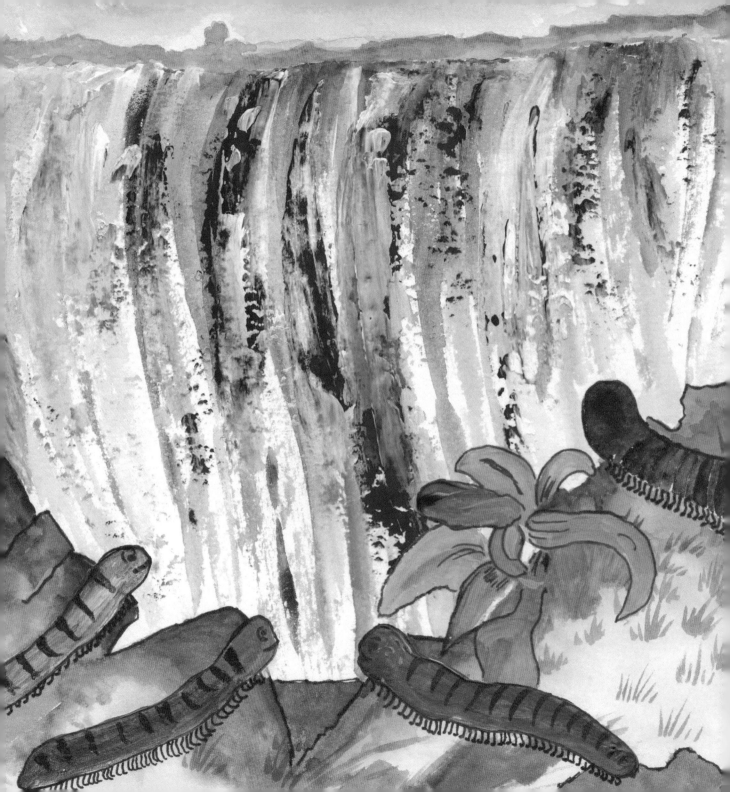

Her father rushes forward.

But too late.

Everybody looks horrified, and stares into the river rushing through the gorge far below them.

Charlie watches this terrible accident.

Then he sees that the young chongololo has landed on a small ledge.

But how long can she stay there without falling off?

Then Charlie's hopes rise.

The grey bird comes flying up the river.

"Mr Lourie, please rescue that little one on the ledge!" he shouts.

The bird takes one quick look.

Then he flies away to the other side of the gorge.

In desperation Charlie looks around.

Suddenly he sees Micky coming through the bushes.

"Please help us rescue little Chipo! You can easily climb down the cliff," pleads Charlie.

The monkey glances into the gorge.

"Very sorry, Charlie, but I am not feeling well today," he replies.

And he skips away.

Charlie realises he must do something.

Then he has an idea.

Quickly he explains to the group what they must do.

One chongololo holds onto a small bush at the top of the cliff.

One by one, the others crawl over each other to make a chain into the gorge.

Eventually the chain reaches down to the ledge.

Charlie then climbs down to the little one, who is crying with fear.

"Hold onto me!" he tells the frightened youngster.

Slowly he climbs back up to safety with Chipo on his back.

Finally the family is together again.

The mother and father are so relieved and happy.

Everyone thanks Charlie.

"Why don't you all come to my house?

We can have a celebration picnic," suggests Charlie.

And so they have a lovely meal outside Charlie's front door.

"Three cheers for Charlie!" says the father.

"Hip hip hooray, hip hip hooray, hip hip hooray!"

"See you again!" says Charlie.